THE CASTLE OF THE PEARL

Dear Joy — This book is part of my
plan in giving you a "gift of Time."
Please take this with my love —
I know that you will fill your
Castle with Pearls!!
Much Love Dear Sister
Dodie

THE CASTLE OF THE PEARL

CHRISTOPHER BIFFLE

Harper & Row, Publishers
New York, Cambridge, Philadelphia, San Francisco
London, Mexico City, São Paulo, Singapore, Sydney

This book is
dedicated to
my mother and father

FIRST EDITION

Designer: Abigail Sturges

Illustration on page 15 is by Rick Chavez.

Library of Congress Cataloging in Publication Data
Biffle, Christopher.
  Castle of the pearl.
  1. Self-actualization. I. Title.
BF637.S4B5   1983   158'.1   82-48248
ISBN 0-06-464057-4 (pbk.)

---

85 86 87 10 9 8 7 6 5 4 3 2

CONTENTS

INTRODUCTION

THIS IS A BOOK to help you see your life more clearly. Inside the Castle you are about to enter, you will find all of the important people of your life. You will have the chance to think about where you have been, where you are now, where you are going. You will need a pen.

Read slowly and let the images, memories, answers and responses form themselves. What exactly do I mean? To say more would spoil your journey.

I thank Jan Collins and La Rosa Faust for their typing, Ada Lee Mattison for her Latin, Hilda Moskowitz and Fred Burgess for their comradeship, Pascual Oliva for help in a small emergency, Jeanne Flagg and Irv Levey for their guidance and Susan Killikelly for her copy editing.

I have too much to thank my wife, Deidre, and my daughter, Persephone, for. If this castle is about love, then they are my guides.

chapter 1
THE GREAT HALL

t is long ago. It is a morning in Spring and you are walking up a dirt road that is still wet with the dew toward a gray Castle on a hill. The fields on each side of the road are dark, newly plowed and orderly. To your right, they stretch far away toward green hills. To your left, they stop abruptly at the edge of a great forest. The trees are near enough that you can hear larks singing.

Even though it is early, there are men, boys and oxen in the fields. You turn and see curling plumes of smoke above the chimneys of the village they have left. Beyond the town are vineyards that mount in neat squares up into the hills below snowy mountains.

You walk carefully on the center ridge of the road above puddles of water in the deep ruts. There are bright blue and white banners flying from every turret of the great Castle before you. You can see men pacing the battlements and looking out over the countryside. They are still too far away for you to see their faces.

You enter a row of trees, hazels, planted on each side of the road for several hundred yards below the Castle. They are huge and very old. Their limbs cross high in the air above your head. It is still early Spring, and as you look up, you see green leaves sprouting at the ends of the slimmer branches and twigs.

The road curves upward through these ancient trees. As you climb, you watch the tower at the center of the Castle. It is much taller than the corner towers and is made of older or darker stone. There are narrow windows cut in its sides, and you imagine that if you stood on top you'd be able to see the whole world.

You look up the ancient aisle of trees toward the gateway. You see a figure standing on the road some distance below the Castle. The figure stands with arms crossed, looking down the hill toward you.

First you see this is a man, and when you are closer, you see it is an old man. Standing before him, you can tell he is full of vigor. He is old, but broad-shouldered, steady, clear-eyed and smiling slightly.

He says to you, "My name is William FitzOsbern and I am the Guide of the Castle of the Pearl. Who and what are you?"

You reply, " _____

_____ ."

The Spring air is full of the singing of morning larks. You hear men and boys shouting in the distant fields at their oxen. The air is fresh, crisp and clear.

The Guide then says, "In this Castle you will see where you have been in your life, where you are now, and where you are going. You will see your life and your relationships more clearly. If you could find anyone in the Castle, who would it be?"

You answer, " _____

_____ ."

The old man smiles. He turns and walks up the pathway toward the ornately carved gate, and you follow. You notice there is a strange emblem sewn into the back of his cape. As you draw closer, you see the same design carved into the stone archway. It is _____ .

The Guide turns and stands beneath this emblem and says somewhat formally to you, "I welcome you to the Castle of the Pearl." You reply that you have come a long way, and he smiles again and says that he is happy you have come. There is something in him that you trust.

He turns and you follow him into the Castle. You see a large paved courtyard before you, but he turns to the right and you follow him into a small room built into the arch of the gateway. Here there is a mirror with a carved wooden frame, an iron-bound chest, a basin of water and clean linen, and, on a sturdy table in the center, a leather-bound book. He motions you toward the basin of water, and you wash the dust from your face. When you rub your wet hands on your face and the back of your neck, something in you feels alive that you haven't felt since childhood. You dry your face on the rough, clean cloth and, for some reason, cannot keep from smiling. You say, "＿＿＿＿＿＿＿

＿＿＿＿＿＿＿＿＿＿＿＿＿＿＿＿＿＿＿＿＿＿＿ ."

He looks at you for a moment. "The Castle has been prepared for your visit. In your three days here, it is yours. It is a place for you to rest, reflect and gain clarity for your journey into the future."

He opens the iron-bound chest and brings out a robe that someone born of noble blood would wear. It is beaded with pearls and small opals. As you put it around your shoulders, you look more closely at the design on the front. It is very beautiful. It reminds you of something you saw long ago in a dream.

William FitzOsbern hands you a pair of sandals worked with gold braid. They fit your feet perfectly. Finally he gives you the leather-bound book and says, "Look closely at these pages."

You open the stiff, heavy book. Many of the pages are blank, with ornate borders. You see something strange on the first page. The words are, "It is long ago. It is a morning in Spring and you are walking up a dirt road that is still wet with the dew . . ." You turn the page and come to the words that you are reading right now.

You feel lightheaded. You are reading these words from a heavy leather-bound book standing in a room built into the gateway of the Castle of the Pearl. You hear the Guide speaking the following sentences as you read them: "This journal is a record of your stay here. You will learn many things, but you must teach them to yourself. I must repeat this. Everything you will learn will come from you and not me. I am only the Guide. The Castle, the adventure and the vision you gain will come from your own efforts."

You are not sure you understand what he has said, but you can tell its importance from his tone. He hands you a white quill.

"There are many things you will wish to record in the blank pages of the journal. When you leave the Castle, I will take everything from you but what you have written. The quill is from the Winter Crow. There is no other like it. If the writer wishes, it will write rivers of words and all of them true. Let us begin!"

He leads you over to a mirror that is carved all around its frame with peacocks, doves and coiling grapevines.

"Look into this mirror," says the Guide.

You look at yourself and it is like seeing your face for the first time. It is almost like seeing a stranger, but not quite. The Guide says, "Write now with your white quill what you see in the face before you in the mirror."

You look very carefully at your face and you slowly write what you see

there. _____

_____

_____

_____

_____ .

Now as you look in the mirror, the figure you see begins to speak on its own. It describes in a list of short statements who you are. It says, "I am

_____ ;

and I am _____ ;

and I am _____ ;

and I am _____ ;

and I am _____ ;

and I am _____;

and I am _____;

and I am _____;

and I am _____;

and I am _____;

and I am _____;

and I am _____;

and I am _____;

and I am _____."

Next the Guide leads you into the large, paved courtyard. It is filled with people. From their clothing, you can tell that they have come from many places. There are babies, toddlers, young boys and girls, slender youths and delicate maidens, men and women in their prime, grandparents and some so old you cannot guess their age.

As they turn their faces toward you, many smile; a few toward the back of the crowd show no emotion. There is no face in the courtyard that you do not recognize. Those standing closest to you are your family and others you deeply love. Behind them are your friends. There are some faces from the past that you have not seen in many years. There are some standing before you that have died, but you feel no fear. Farther back in the crowd, you see some that were very important to you once, some that you knew only casually and a few that you only saw in passing. The Guide motions you to open your book to the first blank page. The page is headed "The Faces in the Courtyard." He bids you write.

You take the feather of the Winter Crow and list the names of the people standing in the crowd that strike you most vividly. You write a word or phrase for those whose names you can't remember.

You begin with your family.

THE FACES IN THE COURTYARD

When you are finished, the Guide says, "You may invite no more than nine into the feast in the Great Hall. Everyone will be fed, but invite those to your table inside that are important to you or that you wish to speak with. Some may be members of your family, some may be people you haven't seen for a long time. In this magical Castle you may even invite those that have passed away; this will cause you no fear or discomfort." You call out the following names in the courtyard:

_____   _____

_____   _____

_____   _____

_____

                _____

You walk into the Great Hall. There is a large, rough-hewn table in the middle, surrounded by nine chairs with a throne-like chair at the head. Windows cut high in the walls let in pillars of Spring light. At the far end of the room is a fireplace that seems large enough to burn a tree in.

The Guide stops you and your guests and says, "Since you are the host, you must decide where everyone is to sit. Turn to the diagram in your journal and write in your guests' names next to their chairs. The seats on your right and left and directly opposite you are places of honor."

You sit down and your guests take their places. Two musicians enter the hall, one carrying a mandolin and the other a flute. They begin to play. Your guests listen. One taps a finger quietly on the table keeping time.

The Guide has not taken a seat at the table. He stands quietly behind you now in the position of a servant. He whispers into your ear, "Look very carefully now at each of your guests. These are people that you've chosen from everyone in the world to share this feast with. Look at each person in turn and write in your journal whatever images, memories, words or feelings occur to you about each one."

14

The Feast in the Great Hall

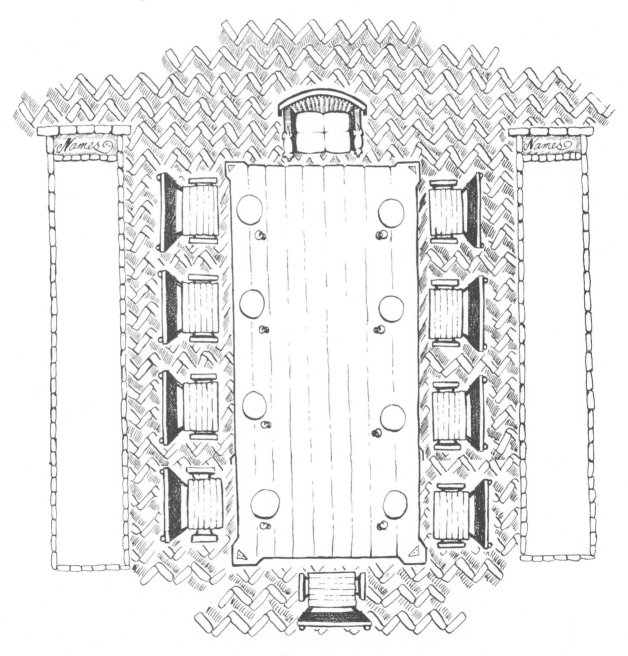

LOOKING AT MY GUESTS

GUEST 1

GUEST 2

GUEST 3

GUEST 4

GUEST 5

GUEST 6

GUEST 7

GUEST 8

GUEST 9

Your reverie is interrupted when the music finishes.

You look at your guests, clap your hands and call out merrily, "Let the feast begin!"

Immediately servants stream into the Great Hall carrying platters of roast duck, pheasant, guinea hen, great plates of trout and perch, bowls of small new potatoes, fresh bread shaped like crosses and shields, pitchers of beer, wine, mead, sweet water and fresh milk, a cunning pastry shaped like a castle complete with moveable drawbridge, hens and pigs carved out of sugar. Two servants carry in a whole roast boar and walk around the table as the guests applaud. Three more mandolin players enter and there is a ceaseless music of conversation and laughter as the plates of food and pitchers of drink go round and round the table. No one's goblet is allowed to remain empty for a moment. Rare cheeses and gleaming fruit are brought in. A great pie is placed in the center of the table, and when it is cut, wrens fly out and everyone shouts. Some guests get up and begin to sing with the musicians, others push themselves back from the table and roll their eyes toward the ceiling. Finally the last guest is finished and all are too full and too happy to move.

You look into their flushed and happy faces. The Guide whispers that it is now time for you to speak. He tells you to think about each of your guests and say, briefly, to each what you have always wanted to say. No guest in the Castle can be hurt by the Truth.

You pause and look carefully at each face turned toward you. You feel calm. Going from guest to guest you say what you have always wanted to say.

SPEECHES TO MY GUESTS

GUEST 1

GUEST 2

GUEST 3

SPEECHES TO MY GUESTS

GUEST 4

GUEST 5

GUEST 6

SPEECHES TO MY GUESTS

GUEST 7

GUEST 8

GUEST 9

chapter 2
THE ROOM OF MAPS

HE FEAST IS OVER NOW, the guests have gone to their rooms and you are alone with the Guide in a small chamber full of maps and strange measuring instruments. The books stacked along the walls are very old and dusty. There is a huge yellow globe in one corner and a thick, beautifully woven rug on the floor. What strikes you most about this room is its silence. You feel that any thought you had here would be perfectly fresh and clear.

William FitzOsbern spreads a parchment map on the table and looks at you. For the first time in your visit, you look carefully at his face. He is old but there is still a Spring light in his eyes. His features seem sturdy and well carved and have none of the weakness that you see in many of the faces of people you know. His eyebrows are gray and wiry. His forehead is clear of tension and worry. The bones of his cheeks and jaw are strongly carved and firm. He has the well-molded and noble features that you would find on an ancient coin.

There is something curious about the map he has spread before you. Drawn on the parchment is something that looks like two ladders or two rows of boxes. On one side is the date of your birth. It is ＿＿＿＿＿＿＿.

The Guide says, "Here you will begin to learn how to draw your Lifemap. Every life follows many paths. You have been on one path with your mother, on another with your father, on still others with your friends. On this first map I would like you to make a record of two paths: the Path of Important Events and the Path of Places. You see each path is divided into the same boxes: Early Childhood, Late Childhood, Adolescence, Early Adulthood and Adulthood. First think about the Path of Important Events. Write down words or phrases that identify important events in your early childhood. Perhaps your earliest memories are of some significant event; you may want to note any marriages, births, deaths, traumas or joys that occurred in these early years. Then go on to the next box, the next stage on this path, to Late Childhood. What important events do you remember from these years of your life? Decide for yourself what is important: a special birthday or Christmas, the purchase of a pet, a new job for one of your parents, or perhaps some larger issues like a political event that somehow touched your life or your family. Write down words or phrases that help you see the Path of Important Events through your whole life from birth until today. When you have finished that, the next path, the Path of Places, will be easy to complete. Here, simply record the places you lived and, if you wish, the important places you visited from your earliest years to the present. You would begin with the city you were born in; you would end with the city you left before coming to the Castle. You could include addresses and words or phrases that remind you of the houses you lived in, vacations you had. Perhaps you spent a summer or a holiday somewhere that was important to you. Record these important places at the proper place on the path. You may even wish to identify them more accurately with a year. Work at this as long as it gives you pleasure.''

And so you begin to work in this marvelously quiet room, sketching out two paths on the map of your life. At first you are surprised at how many blanks there are and how uncertain you are of the dates, but as you work longer on the map, things occur to you that you hadn't thought of for years. You enter the names of people that are associated with important events. You make brief notes about experiences with family members and loved ones, you locate the important peaks and valleys, the places you lived and visited on the two roads of your past. You work slowly and thoughtfully far into the night.

TWO PATHS ON MY LIFEMAP

	EARLY CHILDHOOD	LATE CHILDHOOD
PATH OF IMPORTANT EVENTS		
PATH OF PLACES		

ADOLESCENCE	EARLY ADULTHOOD	ADULTHOOD

chapter 3
THE SLEEPING CHAMBER

OU'RE ALONE NOW in your chamber after spending your first day in the Castle of the Pearl. Your bed has a canopy and painted on the inside are stars, moons and angels. There is one candle burning in the corner and a servant outside the door. The room is faintly scented with rose water, and you feel warm and completely comfortable. The map that you have begun to make of your life fascinates you. You begin to see the jumble of memory laid out in an orderly way, but you know you have much more work to do. You reach over to the night stand and pick up your journal and the quill of the Winter Crow. You open to the page that is headed "List for a Letter to the Most Important Person in My Life" and you know what you should do.

Before you write, you think about this person that has touched you very deeply. Your life would have been different without this relationship.

There's much more you want to say to this person than you could have said at the feast. Before you write the letter in your journal, you make a list of memories, images, words and feelings, just as they come out of the quill of the Winter Crow. This will help you write the kind of letter you really want to write. The list contains brief notes about the close times in the relationship and about the times of difficulty or separation. It contains memories that will help you understand the major stages of the relationship. The list is not an outline or a paragraph or an essay. It is just a list of things that occur to you as you think about this extremely important person. Alone in your chamber, late at night, with only one candle burning, you make the list.

26

LIST FOR A LETTER TO
THE MOST IMPORTANT PERSON IN
MY LIFE

You look over this list, and perhaps if it isn't long or rich enough, you add more to it. There are items on the list that you hadn't thought of for some time.

You go down the list now and circle the items that you want to write the most about in your letter. You think of your letter as your heart speaking and holding nothing back.

This letter will be a place where you can see the relationship more clearly than you ever have before.

LETTER TO
THE MOST IMPORTANT PERSON
IN MY LIFE

LETTER TO
THE MOST IMPORTANT PERSON
IN MY LIFE

chapter 4
THE COURTYARD OF LEISURE

OU OPEN YOUR EYES and it is a chill and fresh morning in the Castle of the Pearl. You feel more like you are coming to life than waking up. You walk shivering across the cold floor toward the window and hear bells somewhere and a boy singing. Out the window you can see the servants down in the courtyard feeding the geese and carrying in armloads of branches. In the distance, there is the village, then there are green hills below snowy mountains. Everything looks as crisp and clear as stones in a cold stream.

You call in the servant and in steps a lively young man with a pitcher of water and clean, brightly woven garments. You dismiss him, dress and begin to hum a tune to yourself. You make a small fire in the fireplace and stand with your back to it until you are warm.

You see your journal where you left it last night on the table. You look at what you have written and you stand in the morning light thinking about it.

The boy has stopped singing outside and is now whistling. You walk over to a small table and see the image of a woman in a walled garden carved on the top. You put the journal down and turn to the next page. It is headed "The Path of My Relationship with the Most Important Person in My Life." At the right end, you put in the date of the last time you saw this person. At the left end of the box or path, you put in the year, and the month, if you can, of your earliest memories of this person. You think about the letter you wrote and the list of images and memories. You begin to fill in this map with short words and phrases that show what happened between the two of you and when it happened. You decide to make this path more detailed than the first two and put in your own little symbols for mountain peaks to stand for the best, highest places in the relationship, and you draw a little symbol for valleys to show where the low points were. You put in walls or bridges or jagged lines to show where the relationship went through its largest changes. You fill in places, houses, cities, vacation spots that bring back memories. You begin to see which were the very closest times and also the times when you were the furthest apart. Perhaps you begin to see a pattern.

THE PATH OF MY RELATIONSHIP WITH

(Divide boxes into years and/or major stages in relationship; write in short phrases that identify important events and memories.)

BEGINNING OF THE RELATIONSHIP

DATE OF
FIRST
MEETING:

MIDDLE STAGES OF THE RELATIONSHIP *Continued*

THE MOST IMPORTANT PERSON IN MY LIFE

MIDDLE STAGES OF THE RELATIONSHIP

DATE OF
APPROXI-
MATE
MIDDLE
OF
RELATION-
SHIP:

NOW

DATE OF
MOST
RECENT
MEETING:

Once you've finished, you hear a knock at the door. You call out, "Enter." You're happy to see the Guide. He is dressed in a long blue robe that is made of a rich and heavy material. He says with a smile that it is time for the morning meal, and you ask if your guests will be there.

He replies, "No, we have other work to do." You follow him down a hall, then through a doorway and down a winding flight of stairs. From the window set into the stairwell, you can see the countryside beyond and the courtyard **below, where you had entered the day before.** A flock of pigeons, **like a single** large animal, sways through the air and then disappears beyond the Castle wall. The Guide leads you out onto a small balcony overlooking a closed courtyard that you have not seen before. A small table is set with the morning meal.

The courtyard is full of servants who are bringing armloads of toys, games and balls, all of which are strangely familiar to you. As you eat and watch the servants below, the Guide explains "This is the Courtyard of Leisure. Here we will assemble the articles which took up your time most entertainingly as a child and adult."

You see a bald servant carrying some of the toys from your earliest child-

hood. They are _____

_____ .

Other toys you see brought in are _____

_____ .

You feel _____

_____

_____ .

    "We have, in fact," FitzOsbern says with a smile, "everything that you've ever owned in your life in large storerooms beneath the courtyard of the Castle. What you are to do this morning is tell the servants what other objects you wish them to retrieve."

    You open your journal to a page headed "The Path of Leisure" and jot down games, toys, activities, books, even movies and TV shows that have given you most pleasure since childhood. You group them according to the stages of your life. Then you stand up on the small balcony and look down into the upturned faces of the servants who are eager to obey your directions.

    You ask the Guide, "What about _____,

one of my favorite TV programs, and _____,

my favorite movie?"

    He says, "To represent all such things, we will bring old newspaper advertisements and copies of *TV Guide.*"

    You both laugh.

    You call out to them each item on your path, and they rush from the courtyard to get it from the storerooms.

THE PATH OF LEISURE

EARLY CHILDHOOD	LATE CHILDHOOD

ADOLESCENCE	EARLY ADULTHOOD	ADULTHOOD

You sit down and eat a bit longer, and the Guide asks you, "What do you think of your stay so far in the Castle?" You reply, " _____

_____ ."

The Guide then says, "What have you learned, if anything, that is of value to you?" You think for a moment, and then you answer, " _____

_____ ."

The Guide asks, "Is there anything that has surprised you so far?" This question is a bit more difficult, but you answer, " _____

_____ ."

Soon the servants return and stand in a confused line. The Guide says, "Have those who are bearing objects from your earliest days stand here beneath us and those who are holding objects that have given you the most pleasure recently stand at the far end of the courtyard. Arrange the other servants to correspond to the years in between. Call out your instructions to the servants so that they line up in a great living map of your leisure."

You follow the Guide's instructions. When you have finished, you see before you the strange spectacle of how you have spent your life when you have been able to do as you wish.

The Guide says, "Let us think about this path together. What is your first reaction to seeing all these things arranged in this way?"

You reply quickly, " _____

_____

_____ ."

"What regrets, if any, do you have when you see how you spent your free time?"

You answer, " _____

_____

_____ ."

"Which of the activities that you see in the courtyard below do you think says the most about who you really are?"

"That is a very interesting question," you reply. "Of everything I see below me, I would choose _____

_____

as closest to my real nature."

"Why is that?"

Again, you think for a moment. Then you reply, " _____

_____ ."

"Which of these, if any, has been the greatest waste of your time?" asks the Guide.

You answer, " _____ ."

"Are you sure?" the Guide asks. You give him your reasons. " _____

_____

_____ ."

"If this line could extend into the future," the Guide says, "what new activities would be out there?"

Your answer is, " _____

_____ ."

"Now look one more time at this living map of your leisure," the Guide says, "but this time imagine that you are looking at what a stranger has spent an entire lifetime doing, as play. What would you say about that person? What characteristics do you see in such an individual? What values? What needs? What drives?"

You answer, " _____

_____

_____ ."

"Do you see," says the Guide, looking at you intently, "that play is really a very serious activity?"

You reply, "_____
_____
_____."

Then you continue thoughtfully to describe what the activities represented in the courtyard below say about the stranger.

You say, "The person I see below me clearly values certain kinds of things, and they are _____
_____
_____.

This person has certain needs, and I think they are _____
_____
_____.

This person is driven by certain serious and not exactly playful drives, and they are _____
_____.

The changes I can detect in this person's life occur in the years _____.

They represent _____
_____
_____
_____.

Finally, if all I knew about the person was what he or she did with leisure time,

I would say that the person _____

_____

_____

_____ ."

You have finished your breakfast and your evaluation of your Path of Leisure. William FitzOsbern says, "It is quite obvious what we should do next."

"Of course it is."

"But I will give you a few moments to relax."

You look up into the morning sky and see small clouds. There is a crow carving designs in the air. The sun is not shining directly into the courtyard, and you are neither too cold nor too warm. It is still early and the light is fresh and almost alive. You have the delicious feeling of alertness and readiness that you had as a child.

The Guide rubs his nose and says, "Are you ready for the next task?"

You nod and answer, "Of course, let us now make a map of work."

You take the quill of the Winter Crow and fill in the Path of Work you find in your journal with everything you've done for a living. You also add the jobs you've dreamed of doing since childhood. The quill makes a river of words. You delight in seeing everything set out this way and you are beginning to understand what the stay in the Castle will do for you.

You write down the first things that you wanted to do when you were a child and understood there was such a thing as work waiting for you. You write down what you said when people asked you what you wanted to be when you grew up. You write down jobs that always appeared attractive to you; you write down the first paying job that you ever held and the jobs you had after that. You also write down anything that has seemed even briefly appealing and which you have rejected. Then you begin to think about the future. You write down any job you can imagine yourself enjoying.

PATH OF WORK

EARLY CHILDHOOD	LATE CHILDHOOD	ADOLESCENCE

EARLY ADULTHOOD	ADULTHOOD

You show the completed path to your Guide.

He says, "Let me ask you a few questions about your map." You answer, smiling, "I am beginning to understand your ways here in the Castle. But I would prefer that you didn't ask me questions when I know more or less what I ought to be doing."

The Guide raises his eyebrows in surprise but then smiles and nods his head and says, "Perhaps you will leave this Castle with a rare gift."

You say, "What I'm going to do is write a letter to myself about what I thought work would be like as a child, what I have always wanted out of work, what I dreamed I would do for a living and what I have actually done for a living. I want a chance to think about what work has done to my inner self, what I wanted it to do and what it might possibly do in the future. In this letter, I'm also going to tell myself about my most important relationships with people I have worked with. I'm going to consider the ways I have failed in these relations and the ways I have succeeded. I want to think about what kind of person I am, what skills and abilities I have and whether or not what I have chosen for a living will realize the unique abilities I was born with. I am going to do all these things and I'm going to do them slowly and carefully, just as they occur to me."

The Guide bows, "Then I will leave you in your thoughtful silence." And so he leaves. You pick up the quill and open your journal. You smile at what you find waiting there.

LETTER TO MYSELF ABOUT WORK

Date _____

Dear _____,

    The first thing I ever wanted to be was _____
_____

because _____
_____.

When I remember that now, I think _____
_____
_____.

    Other things I wanted to be as a child were _____
_____
_____.

I'm not sure what that means about me; perhaps it shows that _____
_____
_____.

    My mother was _____
_____.

What did I think about this? I guess I thought _____
_____.

My father was _____
_____.

What I thought about this was _____
_____.

I'm not sure what influence they had on me, but maybe _____
_____
_____
_____.

LETTER TO MYSELF ABOUT WORK

When I was older I thought of being _____

_____

because _____

_____ .

What I wanted from life then was _____

_____

_____ .

Now, I think _____

_____

_____ .

When I think about all the things I wanted to be, I realize _____

_____

_____

_____ .

The people I've met through work that meant the most to me were _____

_____

_____ .*

*Continue the letter however you wish.

LETTER TO MYSELF ABOUT WORK

chapter 5
THE HALL
OF THE PAST

OU RISE FROM THE MORNING TABLE on the balcony and set off to look through the Castle for William FitzOsbern. You go down the stairwell and come out at a long hallway. You find him stooping down petting a gray and white cat. He nods and leads you down the hall. You see a series of doors labeled with signs in àn ornate writing.

He says, "Each door is a room from your past. The signs are in Latin; I will translate for you." He goes to the first door and reads, " '*Memoria laetissima,*' that's 'happiest memory.' " He walks down the hall translating as he goes. . . .

Memoria miserrima	saddest memory
Tempus magnae commutationis	a time of great change
Plurima celebris memoria	most frequent memory
Memorial de patre	memories of father
Memorial de matre	memories of mother
Memoria de carissima	memories of the beloved
Tempus de viribus	a time of strength
Maturissime memorial	earliest memories
Memoria timidissima	most fearful memory
Porta culpae	door of guilt
Porta perfectionium	door of accomplishments
Tempus aemulationis	time of jealousy

He stands silently behind you. You look back down the dusty, stone-paved hallway, and there are several doorways which you want to enter. You know that you may do as you wish, and unlike most other times in your life, you don't feel the need to hurry. One beautiful thing that you understand about life in the Castle is that there are no clocks. You walk back down the hallway and stop in front of the door from your past that most intrigues you. If you meet someone inside, you know you will want to talk to them. If you see certain scenes from your past, you know you will want to describe them. You and you alone know what is behind each of these doors. The only record you will have of your experience in the room is the one you will keep in the journal with the

quill of the Winter Crow. The doors that you have selected are _____

_____.

Feeling calm and strong, you open the first door, step inside and begin to write about what you see and what happens to you.

DOORS FROM THE PAST

DOORS FROM THE PAST

DOORS FROM THE PAST

DOORS FROM THE PAST

chapter 6

THE BELOVED
AND THE ENEMY

OU LEAVE THE LAST ROOM from your past somewhat tired from the morning's tasks and find the Guide waiting in the hallway. He's holding a goblet carved with cupids and swans, and he says, "Drink this. It is from our spring. It will clear your mind and refresh your spirit. You still have a long way to go."

It tastes like water tastes at the end of a hot day. It is light and clean, almost weightless. You feel your strength return. You are glad there is more to do.

You follow the Guide down the hall and notice for the first time the pattern of the stones laid in the floor. You are walking on a very old mosaic. FitzOsbern notices your interest and says, "The stones in this mosaic were laid in Roman times. Everyone sees a different design here." You look down and decide the mosaic represents ————————————————————

There are two doorways at the end of the hall, both of them iron-studded and sturdy. The Guide turns to you, and as he speaks, he looks almost youthful.

"The door on the left leads to the Room of the Beloved. Waiting for you in this room is the person you have loved most intensely and deeply in your life. The doorway on your right opens into a passageway which leads out to a grassy field for the Battle of Words. If you choose this door, you will meet the person for whom you have the greatest anger—the person who has hurt you most deeply—the person for whom you feel the most bitterness."

You rub your chin and say, "I don't quite understand."

The Guide answers. "It is good that you ask questions now, because I will not accompany you into either of the rooms. I will describe in detail what you are to do whichever door you choose. If you enter the Room of the Beloved, you will record in your journal what you see and everything that you have to say to your beloved. Think back over the history of your relationship, the special and precious times, the way in which it magically formed itself, the times of closest communion. Before you enter, try to remember the important dates and the crucial sequences of events that led to the major stages in your relationship. Perhaps you can bring to mind the exact moment and hour when you fell in love or when you had the greatest and deepest feeling for this person. See if you can recall the dates that accompany the places that are so important to this relationship. List all these things in your journal. Try to see the relationship as a whole from beginning to end and where it is now at this moment in your life."

LIST FOR A TALK
WITH THE BELOVED

The Guide continues, "If you enter this room, here is a plan you may wish to follow:

"First, describe the room and its contents in as much detail as possible. Describe what your beloved is doing and wearing and how you feel upon entering the room.

"Second, begin your heart's speech to your dear one. Begin at the beginning and work through the relationship stage by stage, describing as clearly as you can the important things that happened. The list in your journal will remind you. Examine your strengths and weaknesses in the relationship and those of the other person. Then talk about where you want the relationship to go, about the kinds of things you both can avoid, the kinds of things you both should nurture.

"Finally, when you finish, you may be able to hear your beloved's reply. You should record this also."

ENCOUNTER WITH MY BELOVED

ENCOUNTER WITH MY BELOVED

William FitzOsbern turns toward the other door. "If you decide to enter the room on your right, you must gird yourself for battle. You must think back over the history of this bitter and unhappy relationship. Perhaps there were better, happier times. Perhaps you feel misused or deceived or powerless or cheated. Perhaps you are unhappy with yourself in this relationship. There are many deep and dark things that you have to say here. Before you enter the room, write down some of the things that you want to mention. Do not worry about the order or grammar, just bring your angry weapons into readiness. List everything you want to say in your journal."

LIST FOR THE BATTLE OF WORDS

Your Guide continues, "When you enter, you will walk down a dark passageway toward a light. When you reach the light, you will be at the edge of a grassy field. At the end of the field stands your foe. You will approach each other. Do not allow yourself to get entirely carried away by passion. Calmly and forcefully review for this person the history of the relationship and everything of consequence that went on. Talk about the difficulties and how they mounted and mounted upon each other. Make this a time when you finally say all the things you have to say. Again, try to remember dates and places, try to see things in some kind of order. If you cannot, then simply let your heart roll and let everything inside burst forth. Once you've finished, perhaps you will be able to record what your enemy had to say in response. If you're most fortunate, your enemy will respond to each of your charges."

THE BATTLE OF WORDS

THE BATTLE OF WORDS

chapter 7

THE HALL
OF STATUES

 T IS TIME for the midday meal. You have returned to the Great Hall and have invited a few of your guests to join you. Perhaps you have included some from the courtyard who were

not at the feast. The guests are: _____

_____

_____.

    The Guide is sitting on your right and he whispers to you, "Choose one of your guests to sit on your left that you have not spoken to a great deal or one that you wish to speak to further." The person you choose is: _____

_____.

The Guide looks into your eyes as the servants carry in the dishes. Geese honk in the courtyard.

He asks, "Are you ready for something a little more difficult?" You reply with a laugh, "What I've done so far seems difficult enough. What are you planning?"

"It is time," says the Guide, "for a dialogue."

A servant puts bowls of savory soup in front of you, the Guide and your

chosen guest. Your guest, _____

_____ ,

is leaning forward and listening very carefully to what the Guide is saying.

The others that you have invited to the table are busy with their meals and are watching a juggler with a brown dancing bear.

FitzOsbern says, "I make two suggestions. First, that you record in your journal everything that you and your guest say. Second, that you talk only about serious issues. Ask questions, make observations, recall happy or unhappy memories, seek the truth about the relationship."

You say, "The things I want to talk about with _____

are: _____

_____ ."

Your guest says, "I want to talk about: _____

_____ ."

Then you begin, and you lead the way. You write down what you say and what your guest answers.

DIALOGUE WITH A GUEST

DIALOGUE WITH A GUEST

DIALOGUE WITH A GUEST

The meal is over, you and your guest have finished. The juggler and the bear have left, all your guests have gone hunting for quails' eggs. The Guide leads you through the Great Hall to a small door you hadn't noticed before. Carved on the door is an expressionless face, it looks neither old nor young. The Guide opens the door and you follow him into a small domed chamber that reminds you somehow of a temple or a chapel. There is nothing in the room except a pool of sparkling water.

The Guide says, "This is the Room of the Speaking Air. Any question that is asked here will be truthfully answered."

You are somewhat doubtful, but you say, "Very well, then, I ask the Air what is the date of my birth." And you hear the true reply, _____.

You are startled. You ask a second question, "What, then, is my mother's name?" And you hear the true reply, _____. The Guide says, "I think you understand what is to happen here." You nod your head and he leaves.

There are so many questions you have in your heart. Questions about your past, questions about your relationships, about your present, about your future. And you know for every question, inside you there is an answer if you listen carefully. You understand that in this room you will be able to hear those inner answers. And so you ask questions and hear sensible answers over and over again.

DIALOGUE WITH
THE SPEAKING AIR

DIALOGUE WITH
THE SPEAKING AIR

It is past midday when you have finished the conversation with yourself, in the Room of the Speaking Air. You wander through the Great Hall and find no one but servants and several large, friendly dogs. You are about to go up the winding stairs to your room when you see the Guide. He calls out to you, "Would you care to look at the Hall of Statues?"

Although you are not sure what is in store, you follow him once more. He leads you up a narrow stairway, down short halls, across a balcony above an enclosed courtyard, through several doorways, and up another spiral stairway. You come out in a long room with heavy beams across the ceiling. You had expected to see many statues, but there is only one.

FitzOsbern says, "This is the Statue of your Ideal Self, the one which you would most like to be, the self of your secret and happiest dreams. Approach the statue and walk all around it. Look closely at each part of it for as long as you like. Also note how you feel."

You walk across the room, and as you approach this image of your Ideal

Self, you feel _____

_____ .

You circle it, inspecting it carefully. You spend some time looking at its face. You walk back toward your Guide and he says, "Describe the statue in detail and tell me how you felt while looking at it." You say, " _____

_____

_____

_____ ."

FitzOsbern says, "Very well. Now it is time for you to enter. Walk over to the statue. Stand on the pedestal and your body will become one with it. Then you will be able to do and feel what your Ideal Self can do and feel."

You walk over to the statue. You feel a bit nervous and yet you are drawn to it. You step up on the pedestal and become one with this ideal image of yourself. This is what you feel and this is what happens: _____

_____

_____

_____

_____

_____

_____

_____

_____

Finally you separate from the statue and step down from the pedestal. You return to the Guide. He says, "Tell me what you think about your entire experience." And you reply, " _____

_____

_____

_____

_____

_____

chapter 8
THE FAMILY OF DOLLS

OU ARE WITH YOUR GUIDE once more in the strange Room of Maps, which you were in at the end of the first day. You are sitting at the table with a large Lifemap spread before you. It has eight paths. You look back through your journal and find the map that you made of Important Experiences and Places. You look at the path of your relationship with the most important person in your life. You think back to the living maps of leisure and work that you made, and you read your letter about work. You look at what you wrote in the rooms from your past, and you read either your Encounter with the Beloved or an account of your Battle of Words. You look again at the conversation with your chosen guest at the midday meal. You look at the questions you asked in the Room of the Speaking Air, and you investigate your account of your Ideal Self.

The Guide says, "You have done well thus far. You are learning to see more clearly. There is nothing more difficult or more important than that. Now you are ready to bring many of your paths together into a Lifemap. Look at everything you have done in your journal so far. You have enough information now to fill in seven important paths through your life: Important Events, Places, Leisure, Work, the Most Important Person, Love and Ideals. Select the most significant items from the lists and maps you have already made, add new items as they occur to you. Write in words or short phrases that identify memories, values or experiences along each path. Use the eighth path for anything that doesn't fit on the others. I think you are becoming wise enough now to do all of this without more instructions from me."

You look back through what you have written. You select the most significant items to add to this new Lifemap with Eight Paths. Many new things occur to you. You decide how to word or identify them. You work slowly, carefully, thoughtfully.

LIFEMAP WITH EIGHT PATHS

EARLY CHILDHOOD

IMPORTANT
EVENTS

IMPORTANT
PLACES

LEISURE

WORK

THE MOST
IMPORTANT
PERSON

LOVE

IDEALS

THE EIGHTH
PATH

LIFEMAP WITH EIGHT PATHS

LATE CHILDHOOD

IMPORTANT
EVENTS

IMPORTANT
PLACES

LEISURE

WORK

THE MOST
IMPORTANT
PERSON

LOVE

IDEALS

THE EIGHTH
PATH

LIFEMAP WITH EIGHT PATHS

ADOLESCENCE

IMPORTANT
EVENTS

IMPORTANT
PLACES

LEISURE

WORK

IMPORTANT
PEOPLE

LOVE

IDEALS

THE EIGHTH
PATH

LIFEMAP WITH EIGHT PATHS

EARLY ADULTHOOD

IMPORTANT
EVENTS

IMPORTANT
PLACES

LEISURE

WORK

THE MOST
IMPORTANT
PERSON

LOVE

IDEALS

THE EIGHTH
PATH

LIFEMAP WITH EIGHT PATHS

ADULTHOOD

IMPORTANT
EVENTS

IMPORTANT
PLACES

LEISURE

WORK

IMPORTANT
PEOPLE

LOVE

IDEALS

THE EIGHTH
PATH

When you are finished, the Guide goes over to a small chest, carries it to you and sets it on the floor at your feet. He tells you to open it.

You lift the silver-embossed lid and inside are hundreds of small figures. Some are made of ceramic, some are gold, some are silver, some are sculpted from precious stone or carved from shell, others are simply drawn on pieces of wood. As you pick up each small figure, you are surprised to see that each one bears a likeness to someone you saw in the courtyard on your first day. FitzOsbern says, "Find your mother and father in the chest."

When you sort carefully through figure after figure, you recognize your friends, people that you have loved, teachers, co-workers, and finally your mother and father. You put these on the table before you. Each looks surprisingly lifelike.

The Guide says, "Look carefully at each figure, describe it, and tell how you feel about it."

I look at my mother and see _____
_____
_____
_____
_____
_____
_____
_____
_____ .

I look at my father and see _____
_____
_____
_____
_____
_____
_____
_____
_____ .

William FitzOsbern says, "Look in the chest and please find the baby."

You look through the chest and there, in a white gown, very small and very delicate, is the image of an infant carved from white jade.

FitzOsbern says, "Now we shall play the Game of the Family to help you see more clearly another significant section on the map of your life. The baby is yourself. Imagine the baby has just entered the family. What does the mother say to it and what does she feel?" You reply, "She says, _____

_____

_____ .

She feels _____

_____ ."

The Guide then asks, "What does the father say to you as the baby and what does he feel?"

You reply, "He says, _____

_____

_____ .

He feels _____

_____ ."

The Guide says, "If you are the baby, how do you feel about the mother?"

You reply, "I feel _____

_____ ."

"And the father, how do you feel about him?"

You reply, "I feel _____

_____ ."

"What dangers do you see in this family's future?" FitzOsbern asks.

You reply, " _____

_____

_____ ."

The Guide says, "Find the image of the child." You look through the trunk once more, amazed at how many small figures there are. Finally you find a small child that looks very much like yourself at six or seven. You put it on the table between the image of your father and the image of your mother. It is very strange but interesting to look at these lifelike figures of yourself and your parents. They can almost speak.

The Guide says, "Now, do the same thing you did before. Describe what the mother says and feels toward this young child. Describe what the father says and feels toward this young child and then what you feel as a child toward this family." And you do so.

THE MOTHER, THE FATHER
AND THE CHILD

The mother says: " _____
_____
_____."

The mother feels: _____
_____
_____
_____.

The father says: " _____
_____
_____."

The father feels: _____
_____
_____
_____.

The child says: " _____
_____
_____."

The child feels: _____
_____
_____.

The Guide says, "Now this time go on to other stages. You may proceed as far as you wish. You will find many images of yourself as you grow older. Pick out the images that correspond to crucial years in your life and in your relationship with your mother and father and other family members and see what they are feeling toward you and what you feel about them. You may wish to recreate important events like Christmases, birthdays, weddings, divorces, arguments, vacations, times of darkness or light. Which times from your past would you like to relive through the magical dolls?"

You answer, "_____
_____
_____
_____ ."

"Start with the first and write what each doll says and feels toward the others. If you need other dolls to represent other people, you will find them in the chest. This is a game that can lead to wisdom. Record the scenes that come to mind on the pages of your journal headed "Dialogue of the Family of Dolls."

And so you begin.

DIALOGUE OF
THE FAMILY OF THE DOLLS

SCENE 1

Year (approx.): _____

Dolls present: _____

_____

Situation/Problem: _____

_____

What happens is: _____

_____

_____

_____

_____

_____

_____

_____

_____

_____

_____

_____

_____

_____

_____

_____

_____

DIALOGUE OF
THE FAMILY OF THE DOLLS

SCENE 2

Year (approx.): _____

Dolls present: _____

_____

Situation/Problem: _____

_____

What happens is: _____

_____

_____

_____

_____

_____

_____

_____

_____

_____

_____

_____

_____

_____

_____

_____

_____

DIALOGUE OF
THE FAMILY OF THE DOLLS

SCENE 3

Year (approx.): _____

Dolls present: _____

_____

Situation/Problem: _____

_____

What happens is: _____

_____

_____

_____

_____

_____

_____

_____

_____

_____

_____

_____

_____

_____

_____

_____

_____

DIALOGUE OF
THE FAMILY OF THE DOLLS

SCENE 4

Year (approx.): _____

Dolls present: _____

_____

Situation/Problem: _____

_____

What happens is: _____

_____

_____

_____

_____

_____

_____

_____

_____

_____

_____

_____

_____

_____

_____

_____

chapter 9
TWO GUESTS

OU HAVE JUST FINISHED your wisdom game with the dolls when the Guide re-enters. Following him are your mother and father.

You are surprised for a moment, but as always in the Castle you feel a deep, inner calm. Your parents sit in two chairs against the wall.

The Guide says, "This is an important time. Even though you have thought about your parents previously, now you have a final chance to think about who they are and your relationship with them. Remember, no one in the Castle can be hurt by the Truth. Open your journal and prepare to perform the next task. Your parents will wait peacefully until you are ready to speak to them."

You open your journal and find the words you are reading right now. This is only confusing for a second. You look first at your father. You see a man who

_____

_____

_____

_____

_____.

Then you look at your mother. You see a woman who _____

_____

_____

_____

_____.

Their similarities, or what they hold in common, are _____

_____

_____.

Their differences, or what divides them, are _____

_____

_____.

What is important to your father is _____

_____

_____.

What is important to your mother is _____
_____
_____.

Looking at them both, you see a couple that _____
_____
_____.

You begin to think about your father's past, before you were born. The most important experiences in his life were _____
_____
_____
_____.

This helps you to see him a bit more clearly. When you look at his past, you can see why he _____
_____.

Now, you look at your mother. You think about the most important experiences in her life before you were born. They were _____
_____
_____
_____.

This helps you to see her a bit more clearly. When you look at her past, you can see why she _____

_____

_____.

You stop for a moment. Your father speaks first.
He says, "Please tell me what you feel about me."

You answer, "I feel _____

_____

_____

_____

_____."

He nods. Somehow you can tell that he welcomes the truth.
"When you think about our relationship, what scenes do you see?" he continues.

You answer, " _____

_____

_____

_____."

"Here is a harder question. What do many of these scenes have in common? What do they say about you and me?"

You reply, " _____
_____
_____
_____."

Your father asks, "What do you think I needed most from you?"

You answer, " _____
_____."

"What did you need from me?" he asks.

You say, " _____
_____."

"Is there anything you feel guilty about in our relationship?"

You think for a moment and then answer, " _____
_____."

Then your father says, "Is there anything you think I should feel guilty about in our relationship?"

You choose your words thoughtfully, " _____
_____
_____."

And then you continue your conversation with your father in any way you wish. You talk about the closest times and the most distant times, the peaks and the valleys, how the relationship changed or developed. You both are letting your hearts speak.

94

CONVERSATION WITH MY FATHER

CONVERSATION WITH MY FATHER

Then your mother speaks. "Please tell me what you feel about me."

You answer, "I feel _____

_____

_____

_____."

She nods. Somehow you can tell that she also welcomes the truth.

"When you think about our relationship, what scenes do you see?" she continues.

You answer, "_____

_____

_____

_____."

"Here is a harder question. What do many of these scenes hold in common? What do they say about you and me?"

You reply, "_____

_____

_____

_____."

Your mother asks, "What do you think I needed most from you?"

You answer, " _____

_____ ."

"What did you need from me?" she asks.

You say, " _____

_____ ."

"Is there anything you feel guilty about in our relationship?"

You think for a moment and then answer, " _____

_____ ."

Then your mother says, "Is there anything you think I should feel guilty about in our relationship?"

You choose your words carefully, " _____

_____

_____ ."

And then you continue your conversation with your mother in any way you wish. You talk about the closest times and the most distant times, the peaks and the valleys, how the relationship changed or developed. You both are letting your hearts speak.

CONVERSATION WITH MY MOTHER

CONVERSATION WITH MY MOTHER

You look at your parents.
What you have learned that you want to remember about your father is

_____

_____

_____ .

What you want to remember about your mother is _____

_____

_____

_____ .

What you want to remember about them as a couple is _____

_____

_____

_____ .

chapter 10

THE POSSIBLE SELF

OUR PARENTS and the Guide have left. It is late on your second day in the Castle. You are alone in the Room of Maps with your Lifemap and the chest of dolls. Somehow you are tired of thinking so much about yourself and your relationships. You walk over to the yellow globe in the corner and look at the ancient continents and the ageless seas. You begin to think about what the world was like in the past. The words that seem best to describe the world in

the past are: _____

_____

_____

_____

_____

_____

_____ .

Then you look at the globe and think about the way the world was when you left it, before you began your journey through the Castle. The words that seem best to describe the world you left are: —————————

—————————————————————————————————

—————————————————————————————————

—————————————————————————————————.

You look once more at the yellow globe and you think about the future, the world that you will live in next year and the next and the next. The words that seem best to describe that world are:

—————————————————————————————————

—————————————————————————————————

—————————————————————————————————

—————————————————————————————————.

You leave the Room of Maps, walk out to the Great Hall, and climb the dark and winding stairway to your chamber. You've chosen not to have a meal with your guests on this evening of your second day. You are tired and need privacy for reflection.

You light the candle in your chamber and lie back in the canopied bed with the images of the stars, moons and angels glowing faintly above you. You can hear music and laughter in the courtyard below, but you are glad to be alone. You feel half-awake and you begin to have a strange dream.

In the dream there is an image which fills you with great peace. The longer you look at this image, the more harmony and spiritual contentment you feel. The image has something to do with wholeness and rightness and strength.

There is something naturally correct and strong about it. If you had to describe this marvelous image, you would say: " _____

_____

_____

_____ ."

The image changes and you follow the changes carefully, noting them here.

_____

_____

_____

_____

_____

_____

_____

_____

Next you have an image, a dream image, of yourself. It is not your Ideal Self, nor is it who you are at the present time. It is an image of your Possible Self. This self is one that you could most realistically become. It is a very positive image because it is not born of impossible wishes. It does not reside far in the future. It is the real you, the inner you, the you that you have been before and could be again and feel happiest being. It is the self that has broken through again and again in your life. You see it at different places on your Lifemap, this real inner self. You have felt it in your relationships, especially with those you love, especially at your closest times with them. If you had to describe the image of this Possible Self, you would say: " _____

_____

_____

_____

_____

_____

_____

_____."

    You think now of this Possible Self going through an ordinary day, doing the work that you ordinarily do, meeting the people that you regularly meet. This person, this real inner person, is not impossibly perfect, but acts in a way that gives you the most genuine *peace.* If you had to describe a day in this self's life and the way it related to the important people in your life, you would say: " _____

_____

_____

_____

_____

_____

_____

_____."

chapter 11
LETTERS

OU WAKE IN THE MORNING of your third day at the Castle and something in your heart tells you that this will be one of the most important days in your life. The morning light fills the room and far off you hear the bugle note of a hunter's horn and the distant barking of the dogs. You call in the brightly clad servant and say, "Bring me my breakfast."

The servant nods his head and smiles as if he's made happy by doing anything for you, and darts out.

You sit up in the great canopied bed holding your journal against your knees and think back over your stay these two marvelous days in the Castle of the Pearl. You have written a letter to the most important person in your life, had a dialogue with a special guest, had many of your questions answered, talked to your Beloved, or fought a Battle of Words, and looked at your life with your family, but there are still people in your life that you want to understand more clearly.

You select two people to write letters to this morning. You have become more practiced at this and you are familiar with the procedure. For each person, you make a list of the things you want to say, just as they occur to you. You include memories, images, feelings, things unsaid, needs, experiences, peaks, valleys, times of confusion, times of clarity and joy. You mention the close times and the distant times, the times of celebration, of intimacy, of conflict, of separation, just as they occur to you. You make a river of words with the quill of the Winter Crow.

Once your list has run out, you go back over it and give dates to all the items you can, beginning with your earliest memories of the special person. In your letter you will work forward from these early memories through each crucial stage in the relationship until you reach the last moment that you saw the person. Perhaps you decide to lay your list out on a line that you've marked off with years and months in the same way you learned to do in the Room of Maps. The first date would be the earliest memory; the last date would be the last time the person was in your life.

With your lists and your maps, you are ready to begin letters of reflection about these two important relationships. The servant brings in the breakfast you ordered, and it is, not surprisingly, delicious. You spend your morning writing these two letters. You write carefully but also happily.

LIST FOR A LETTER
TO AN IMPORTANT PERSON

LETTER 1

LETTER 1

LIST FOR ANOTHER LETTER
TO AN IMPORTANT PERSON

LETTER 2

LETTER 2

chapter 12
THE TOWER

ILLIAM FITZOSBERN knocks firmly at your door just as you are finishing your last letter. You feel a certain sadness because you can tell from his face that your time in the Castle of the Pearl is nearly over.

He says, "Now we must ascend the Tower."

You dress and follow him down the hall. The servants have disappeared. You do not hear the chatter of your guests. He goes in a small doorway and then you climb with him stair after stair, higher and higher. You realize that you must be climbing the central tower, the tall one that you saw on your approach to the Castle. As you look out the arrow-slit windows that are cut into the stairwell, the landscape at each turn becomes smaller, more distant, and more precious. You see farther and farther at each level, but the Guide does not pause and you catch only quick glimpses of a maze of roads disappearing into the distance. They all seem to have the Castle as their center.

At last you emerge into a small room at the top of the Tower. There is a mirror-like basin of water in the center of the room. Light streams into the room from two windows that are larger than any you have seen in the Castle thus far. One window is cut into the south wall, the other into the north wall.

The Guide takes you over to the southern window, and you gaze with him across the landscape. There are many paths but one great road. You recognize this as the route that led you to the Castle on your first day. It stretches back over hills, disappears and then appears again, winds through groves of trees, skirts the edge of a glimmering lake and then disappears into distant bluish hills.

"Far off in those hills is the city of your birth, and that main road that you see is the path of all the years of your past," the Guide says. "Every day that you have lived, you have spent on that winding road, passing some of your days in sweet meadows and some in dark storms."

"Look at the map you've made and the road you've traveled. Let us talk for a while about your experiences in the Castle and the road of the past before you write a letter to yourself trying to put all these things into order. What has been your most important experience in the Castle so far?"

You think and then reply, "I have had several important experiences so far. They are: _____

_____

_____

_____."

"What have you learned that you want to remember about yourself or others?" the wise old man asks.

"I want to remember _____

_____

_____

_____."

"As you look back over the road of your past, what are the biggest changes in yourself that you see?"

"I guess I would say _____

_____

_____

_____."

The Guide asks, "Where are the peaks on the road of your past, the highest, most joyful experiences?"

You answer, "_____

_____

_____

_____

_____."

"Now tell me about the valleys, the times of darkness and difficulty."

"The darkest times were _____

_____

_____

_____

_____."

The old man nods. He looks at you for a moment. "What have you learned from darkness, from your pain or difficulties?"

"That is a useful question," you answer. "Perhaps I have learned ____

_____

_____

_____

_____."

"What have you learned from your joy, what have you learned on the peaks of your life?"

"I like that question even better. I have learned _____

_____

_____

_____

_____

_____."

The old man smiles as if he approves of what you have said. Then you realize he has approved of everything you have said and done so far in the Castle. He says, "One important thing I want you to remember about the road of your past and your journal is that, as you have seen, every relationship in your life is a separate path. You have been on one path with your mother, on another with your father, on another with your beloved and others you have loved, on another at play, on another at work. All may have separate peaks and valleys. Of all the paths you have traveled, which do you need to think the most about?"

"I think I understand," you reply. "The paths I need to think the most

about are _____

_____."

"You may want to think about those paths in the letter to yourself which you will soon begin. Tell me this. When you look at your past, do you see any crossroads?"

You reply, " _____

_____."

The Guide asks, "What roads do you see that you should have taken but didn't?"

You answer, " _____

_____

_____

_____

_____

_____

_____ ."

"You have several tasks to complete before you leave this Tower," the Guide says. "First you must write a letter to yourself about this long road that you have come down. Talk about the people that have touched you, that have hurt you, that have made you a better person. Talk to yourself about the conversation we have just had. Expand it in any way you wish. Write about your experiences, the great changes in your life, the peaks and valleys, the victories and defeats. Many of these things you have already looked into, deeply and clearly, in your stay here in the Castle."

You sit down at the small table with your journal. The Guide brings you a bowl of fruit from a small wooden cupboard, and you begin to look back through your journal at your letters, your maps, your conversations and your lists. You want to draw a portrait of yourself with words. Perhaps you do not need now to make a list or any further diagrams. Perhaps everything you have done so far has prepared you for this great feat of memory, analysis and description. You will begin the letter to yourself with your earliest memories. You will talk about the first people that touched you deeply. You will go through each major stage of your life. In separate places in your journal you will find things that you will want to draw together into a single clear whole that stands for the road of your life thus far. It is not an easy task, but you are well prepared, and you feel a certain eagerness to see your whole life clearly. And so you pick up the white quill and begin the letter to yourself about the path you have traveled and its most important features.

LETTER TO MYSELF
ABOUT THE PAST

LETTER TO MYSELF
ABOUT THE PAST

LETTER TO MYSELF
ABOUT THE PAST

chapter *13*

THE UNIVERSE OF OTHERS

HEN AT LAST you put down the quill of the Winter Crow, the Guide comes over to the table. "You have written well," he says. "Of course, there must be some things you have left out. Perhaps at another time you will want to fill them in. But now, look into the Basin of Reflecting Water. You will see who you are now. After your experience these last three days in the Castle you may be able to see more than you did in the mirror."

You look into the sweetly scented water. You look deeply at your own face. You say, "I see a person who _____

_____

_____

_____

_____."

And then you look at the Guide, smile, look back into the reflecting

water and say, "I am _____.

I am _____.

I am _____.

I am _____.

I am _____.

I am _____.

I am _____.

I am _____.

I am _____.

I am _____.

I am _____."

The old man now leans over the basin with you. "If you look even more deeply, you will see where you are now in your life. You will be able to see your present relationships more clearly than you have before, your present strengths and weaknesses, successes and problems."

FitzOsbern steps back and continues, "You are now ready to make a large simple diagram of the present. Imagine for a moment that you are the sun and that the planets circling you are the people that are in your life now. There may be many, many planets stretching out into space or there may be very few. The planets closest to you are the people that are closest to you in your life now. The most distant are the people that are most distant."

And so you open your journal to the next blank page. You make a small circle in the center and label it with your name. Closest to you, you put the dearest ones, and farther away, you put those that are more distant from you. Finally you are looking at the Universe of Others with yourself at the center.

UNIVERSE OF OTHERS

The Guide says, "Now let us make this Universe of Others a bit more complete. Look at each of the planets in your Universe and, as you look at each one, think of words or phrases that describe the positive and the negative things you feel about this person. Place these words and phrases as moons circling each planet."

You do not quite understand. The Guide can tell from your face. He says, "For example, let us say the closest person to you in the Universe of Others is your mother. You have her name on the planet that is circling closest to your sun. When you think of her, words like 'warmth,' 'trust,' 'happiness,' come naturally to mind. Make each of these words a moon or small circle and put them in orbit around her planet. If you have negative feelings, add negative words. Do the same for each of the other planets so that you can see the Universe you live in with others more clearly."

And so you add the Moons of Feeling to your planets.

Later the Guide says, "You have done a good job. Let me ask you a few questions about where you are now in your life and then you must decide if you wish to add more detail to the Universe you are making. First tell me about your worries. What are your biggest ones right now?"

You answer, "_____

_____

_____."

"What are the sources of your greatest pleasure or joy now?" You reply, "_____

_____

_____."

125

"Here is a fine question," the old man says. "What are your most persistent fantasies or daydreams in your life at present?"

"Well," you answer, "_____

_____

_____

_____."

"What are your strongest or most persistent memories?"

You think for a moment and then answer, "_____

_____

_____

_____."

"What are your present strengths?"

You answer boldly, "_____

_____

_____

_____."

"What are your present weaknesses?"

You answer honestly, "_____

_____

_____

_____."

The Guide folds his arms and looks at you. "I have noticed that you have grown more independent. You are becoming your own guide. This is good. Here is a challenge. I have no idea how you'll meet it. Look at the Universe you have created with the Moons of Feeling. Think back about what you have just been saying about your present strengths, weaknesses, memories, day-dreams, joys and worries. You should now decide which of these, if any, to add to the diagram you have made of your life at present. You are the creator. You may add more planets, moons, comets, meteors, or even space dust if you wish to represent a more complete picture of your present situation. Play with your Universe until it looks and feels like the real universe you now live in. What-ever you do, I am confident you will do as you wish."

And you do.

chapter 14

REFLECTIONS

HE LIGHT is beginning to fade in the windows of the Tower. For many hours you have been mapping out your place in the present, yet you feel no hunger for anything except wisdom and clarity.

Your Guide says, "Now if you are clever . . ." And you interrupt him and say, "I am becoming clever."

He continues smiling. "If you wish, write a letter to yourself about where you are now. Use the Universe you have just made in any way that is most useful to you. Tell yourself what you need to hear about your life at present."

LETTER TO MYSELF
ABOUT MY PRESENT UNIVERSE

LETTER TO MYSELF
ABOUT MY PRESENT UNIVERSE

LETTER TO MYSELF
ABOUT MY PRESENT UNIVERSE

chapter 15
THE ROAD OF
THE FUTURE

OU HAVE NOW FINISHED the letter to yourself. The Guide leads you over to the window in the north wall. As the sky fades to twilight, he says, "The road that you see below is the road of your future. If it were earlier in the day, you could see all the way to the horizon. As you look outward now, as the dark is falling, perhaps you will be able to see certain features on the road ahead that you want to avoid and certain parts of the landscape that you want to try to travel through. Sit down now, and write your final letter, a guide to your future. Make your plans in one letter. Give yourself the best advice that you can. Go through each important relationship in your life and see if you can map it some distance ahead. Use all the wisdom and clarity that you've gained in the Castle and in the Tower and tell yourself what you need to hear about these important relationships, about yourself, about your weaknesses and your strengths, about work and play and about the whole landscape which you will

soon be passing through. If you have learned any rules to guide you, if there are any principles that you want never to forget, record them here. If there are things that you have learned about others that could help you in your relationships, write them down. If you see your goals more clearly, then chart out a path to them. If you want to reorganize your daily life or the way in which you relate to others or what your priorities are now at this point in your life, then make a schedule and a map here for yourself in this final letter.''

And so you sit down and think about everything that has happened to you in the Castle of the Pearl and you write one last time with the quill of the Winter Crow, slowly, thoughtfully and carefully, far into the night. You do not even notice that the Guide has left you alone in the Tower. The stars come out dimly and then shine, purely and clearly. The moon rises heavily above the distant hills and then begins to sail across the sky as you write this letter to yourself about your future. Finally, it is dawn and you are finished.

LETTER TO MYSELF
ABOUT MY FUTURE

LETTER TO MYSELF
ABOUT MY FUTURE

LETTER TO MYSELF
ABOUT MY FUTURE

LETTER TO MYSELF
ABOUT MY FUTURE

chapter 16

THE PEARL

 T IS YOUR LAST MORNING in the Castle. Your journal is complete, and you know that you must now go forth. You descend the winding stairs through the fresh morning air. You walk back through the Great Hall. It is being prepared for the feast of another. You hear the roosters crowing outside. You walk out to the great courtyard. All the guests have left on their own roads into the future, and William FitzOsbern, your Guide, meets you there. You look deeply at each other and the Guide says, "I wish you well on every road that you travel."

You say, "_____

_____

_____ ."

He leads you around to the north gateway. Before you is your road, stretching off into the hills. He takes from you the precious robe that you were given on your first day. He asks you to remove the gold-braided sandals. He takes back the quill of the Winter Crow.

He says, "When you arrived, and it seems now long ago, I said that on your last day in the Castle I would take everything from you except your journal. Now, I have changed my mind. I have a small and perhaps precious gift for you."

He places in your palm a small leather pouch drawn tightly with a cord.

You untie the cord and pour down into your palm a single glistening gray-white Pearl.

The Guide says, "This Pearl shall guide you, if you wish it, on all your travels into the future. Keep it with you always and it shall never fail you." You walk out through the gate with the Pearl in one hand and your journal rich with wisdom and clarity in the other. When you are partway down the hill toward your future, the Guide calls out to you his last question, "What is the Pearl?"

You turn back to the ancient man and you say, "—————————

—————————————————————————————

—————————————————————————————

—————————————————————————————

—————————————————————————————————————."

139

HOW TO DRAW
A COMPLETE LIFEMAP

YOU HAVE BEEN DRAWING MAPS and diagrams all the way through your visit in the Castle. Make a grid of large boxes on a piece of paper. Label the boxes across the top "Time" and the boxes down the sides "Paths."

You can make your map as detailed or as general as you wish. One way to begin would be simply to mark each "Time" box as one year in your life. The first box would be a "1" for one year old, the next a "2" for two years old and so forth. The boxes down the sides could then be labeled for whatever paths you want to follow through your life, "Important Events," "Places," "Leisure," or any of the other themes or persons you have investigated or remembered in the Castle. Then inside each box write a few words or phrases that identify that particular path at that particular year in your life. For example, on the bottom of the facing page is a section of a Lifemap someone left behind in the Castle.

As you can see, different kinds of things can be recorded along each path in your life. You may wish to record strong memories, peaks, valleys, feelings, information about life changes, places you lived, close times, distant times. When you really want to look at a part of your life closely, the Lifemap can be made even more detailed by changing the "Time" boxes from years to months, or even days or hours. Here is a list of "Paths" you may want to chart:

1. Father
2. Mother
3. Brothers and Sisters
4. Relatives
5. Friends
6. Teachers/Important or Influential Others
7. Co-workers
8. Bosses or Supervisors
9. Peaks (as you trace them through the years)
10. Valleys (ditto)
11. Relations with God or the Divine
12. Work
13. Play
14. Daydreams or Fantasies (as they develop through the years)
15. Goals (as they change or remain the same)
16. Crossroads (in the year or month they occur)
17. Objects (these play a surprising role in our lives)
18. Christmases (a record of these, as well as Birthdays, might be useful)
19. Important Events (should be located at proper year and month if possible . . . births, deaths, marriages, etc.)
20. Schools
21. Achievements (a record of these might be heartening)
22. Ideals

	TIME				
PATHS	1	2	3	4	5
Father	working in hat factory		earliest memory: tricycle/ hammer		begin base-ball with Dad . . . fear/ joy
Mother	working in school cafeteria			memory: I'm sick; she is wiping my face w/ washcloth	drawing flowers together/ frustration

If there are many paths you want to follow through your life, just use another page with the *same* years but with new paths. For example, someone might be ambitious enough to want to follow fifteen paths through the years ten through fifteen. One page with the "Time" boxes labeled "10" through "15" would be used for seven or eight of the paths, and the next page would be labeled with the *same* years, "10" through "15," and with the remaining paths.

Write whatever words in the boxes you wish along the Lifepath. These should help you identify or remember the event or feeling you want to record. Once completed, you should be able to see your life more clearly than you ever have before. You can then read the map in one of two ways. Select a year and read *down* the page and you will see where you were on all the paths through that year (with your father, mother, best friends and so forth). Select a path and read *across* the pages and you will see how that relationship or Lifepath developed across the years (relations with your father from earliest memory to present, the same with your mother and so forth).

The Lifemap technique can also be used to chart paths into the future. But, one must agree with William FitzOsbern, you will certainly do as you wish. Along with my character, I wish you well on all your travels.

If you would like to share any or all of your Castle experiences with me, or if you have advice or suggestions, I'd like to hear from you.

Christopher Biffle
Philosophy Department
San Bernardino Valley College
San Bernardino, CA 92403